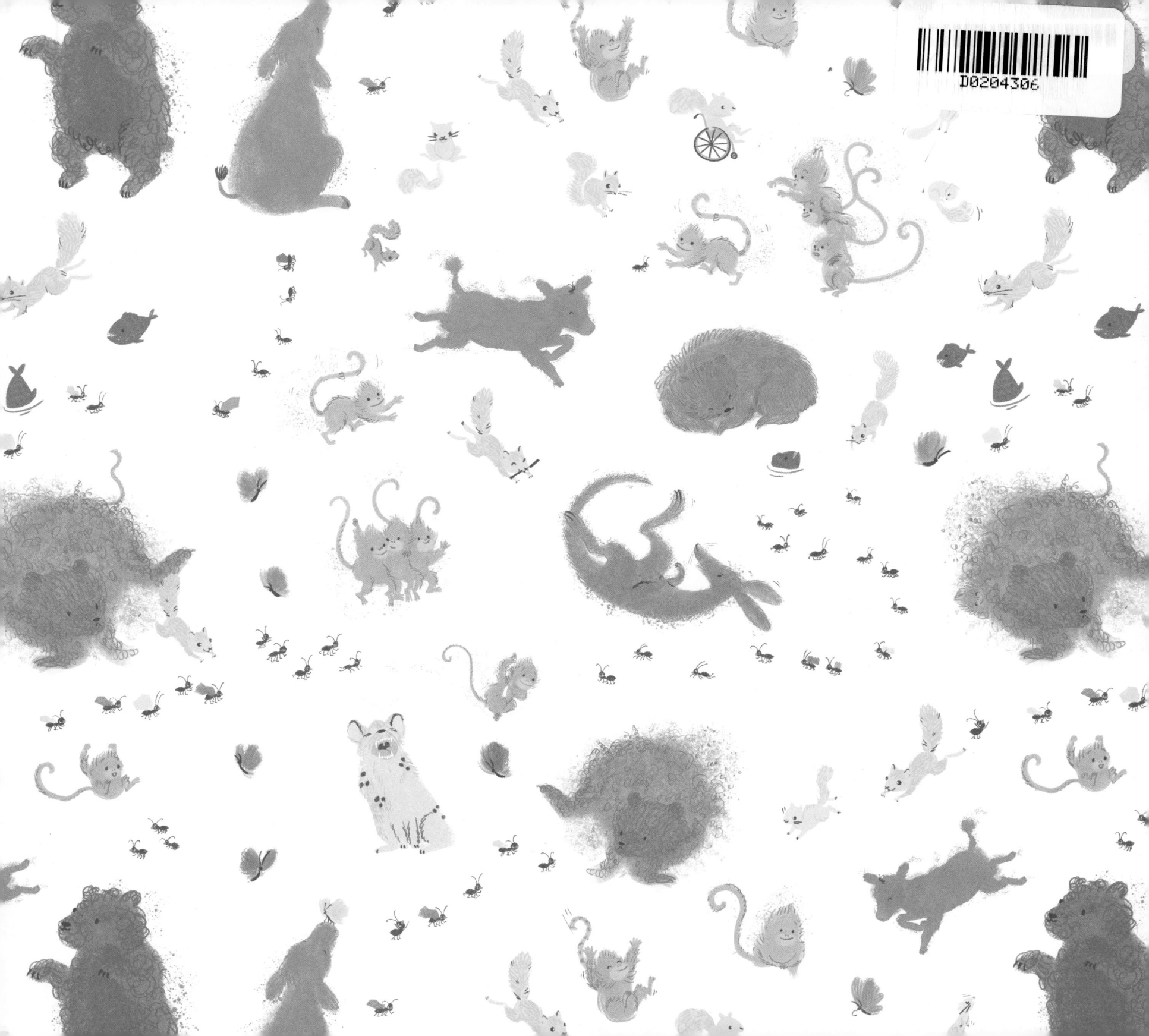

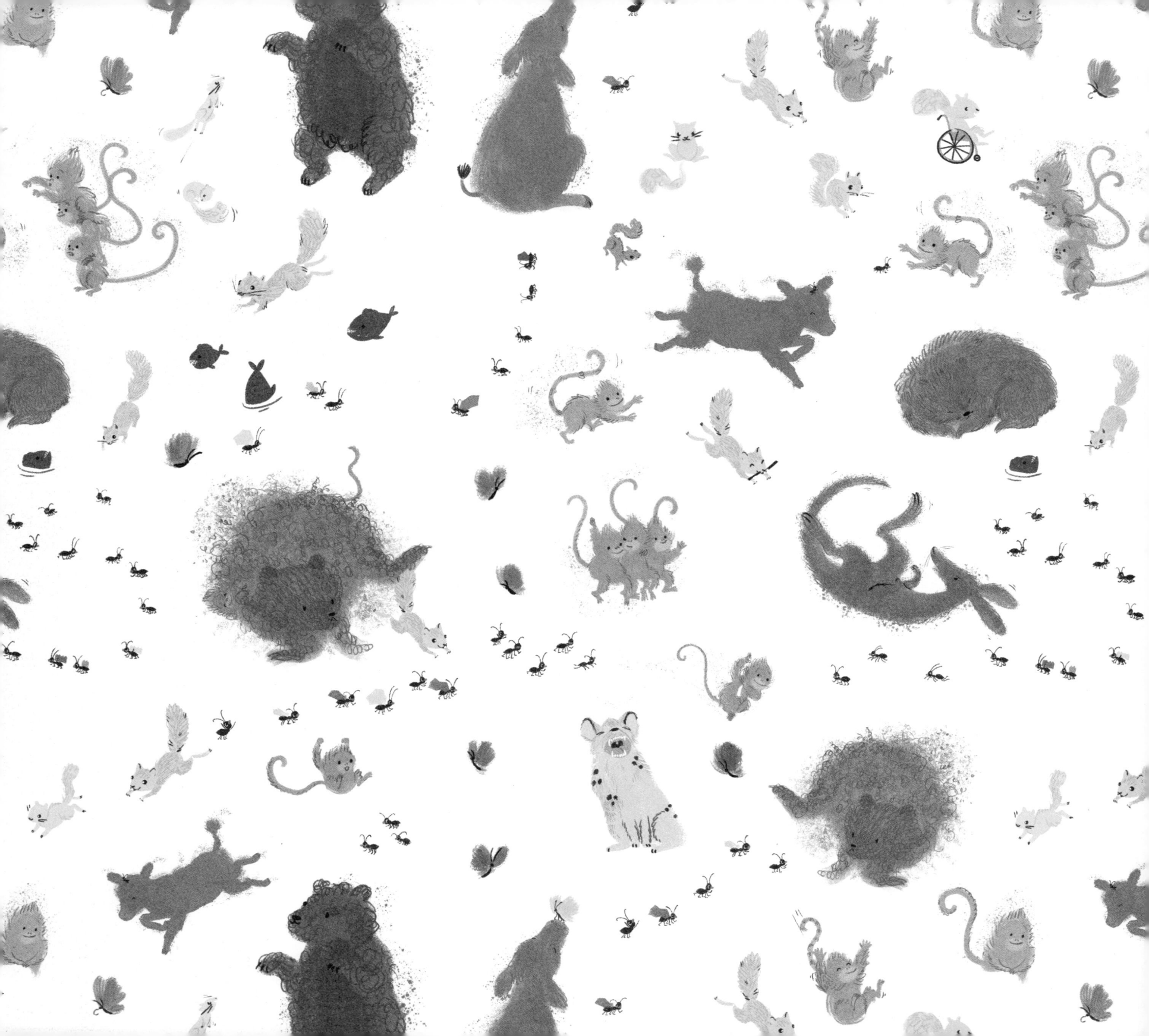

written by
Laura Marx Fitzgerald

illustrated by
Jenny Løvlie

WILD FOR
WINNIE

Dial Books for Young Readers

The teacher said a new kid was joining our class.
But Winnie was no ordinary kid.

At circle time, she howled like a hyena.

At reading time, she kicked like a kangaroo.

And at lunch, she chomped
like a piranha.

But our teacher said, "Here's a wild idea—"

"Maybe Winnie sees and hears and feels the world differently than most of us. So why don't we give her world a try?"

On Monday, Winnie could not stop monkeying around.

So at recess, we joined her on the jungle gym.

On Tuesday Winnie was really antsy.

So we all crawled into cocoons and turned into butterflies.

On Wednesday, she was a bull in a china shop.

So we pulled together
to build something amazing.

On Thursday, Winnie was pretty squirrelly.

So we all went nuts on an obstacle course.

And on Friday Winnie was just a bear.

So we burrowed into a cozy den.

It turns out Winnie *is* an ordinary kid, just like us.
And sometimes we all feel the world differently,

just like Winnie.

You know those kids. The ones who blithely run their scooters into your ankles and knock kids off swing sets, but who melt down at the sound of the vacuum cleaner.

Some call them insensitive. Some oversensitive. Some kids are even diagnosed with Sensory Processing Disorder. Too often their responses to the world around them get them excluded from that world. And when we do include them, it's usually on our terms—not theirs.

The good news is that wise parents, teachers, and therapists have developed simple interventions to help calm the nervous system. Best of all, they feel like child's play.

What follows are some activities you can introduce on a playdate, in the classroom, or on the playground to support "one of those kids"—or really any kid who is having "one of those days."

FOR MONKEY-AROUND DAYS:
Swinging for vestibular regulation and balance

- Have kid lie down in the middle of a sheet, while you and a partner each grab an end and gently lift and sway from side to side.
- Forget the expensive swing set. Add a rope, porch, standing-frame, or tire swing. You can even buy portable hammocks.
- No outdoor space? Add a cocoon swing to your child's bedroom, or even a collapsible doorway swing or pull-up bar. Or just find your way to your local playground.

FOR ANTSY DAYS:
Deep-touch pressure to calm the nervous system

- Burrito bar! Have your child lie down on a blanket and give you "toppings" to add to their burrito. Give taps and light thumps for each topping: drop in beans, mush in guacamole, drum your fingers for grated cheese. Then roll up your child in the blanket like a tortilla (head uncovered, of course!). Unrolling is just as fun.
- Offer your child a backrub. Or roll a large exercise ball or foam roller from head to toe.
- Hugs. Lots of hugs.

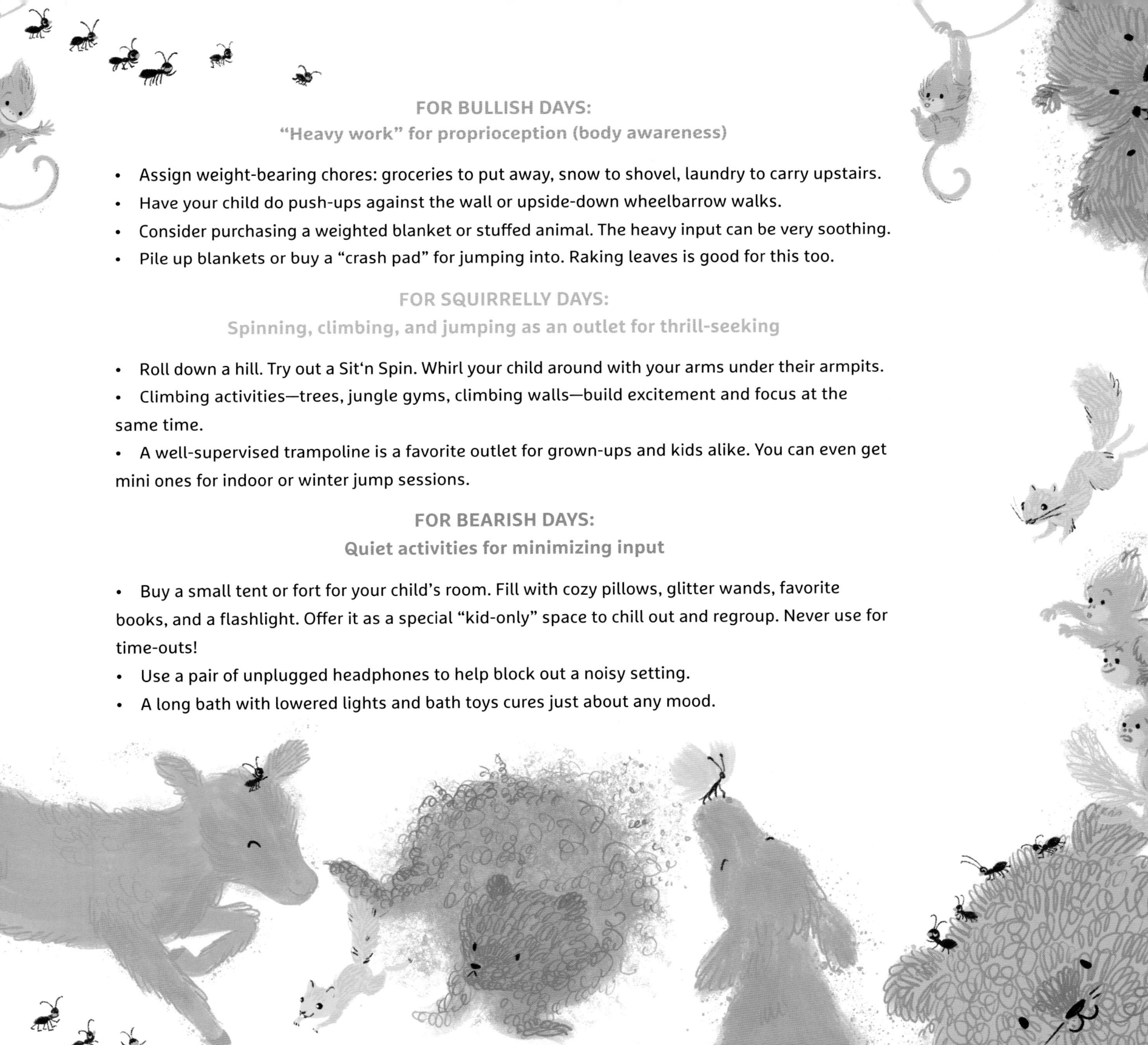

FOR BULLISH DAYS:
"Heavy work" for proprioception (body awareness)

- Assign weight-bearing chores: groceries to put away, snow to shovel, laundry to carry upstairs.
- Have your child do push-ups against the wall or upside-down wheelbarrow walks.
- Consider purchasing a weighted blanket or stuffed animal. The heavy input can be very soothing.
- Pile up blankets or buy a "crash pad" for jumping into. Raking leaves is good for this too.

FOR SQUIRRELLY DAYS:
Spinning, climbing, and jumping as an outlet for thrill-seeking

- Roll down a hill. Try out a Sit'n Spin. Whirl your child around with your arms under their armpits.
- Climbing activities—trees, jungle gyms, climbing walls—build excitement and focus at the same time.
- A well-supervised trampoline is a favorite outlet for grown-ups and kids alike. You can even get mini ones for indoor or winter jump sessions.

FOR BEARISH DAYS:
Quiet activities for minimizing input

- Buy a small tent or fort for your child's room. Fill with cozy pillows, glitter wands, favorite books, and a flashlight. Offer it as a special "kid-only" space to chill out and regroup. Never use for time-outs!
- Use a pair of unplugged headphones to help block out a noisy setting.
- A long bath with lowered lights and bath toys cures just about any mood.

For William
—L.M.F.

For Lisa. I'll always
go wild for you!
—J.L.

Dial Books for Young Readers
An imprint of Penguin Random House LLC, New York

First published in the United States of America by Dial Books for Young Readers,
an imprint of Penguin Random House LLC, 2022

Text copyright © 2022 by Laura Marx Fitzgerald
Illustrations copyright © 2022 by Jenny Løvlie

Visit us online at penguinrandomhouse.com.

Library of Congress Cataloging-in-Publication Data is available.

Manufactured in China • ISBN 9780593111819 • HH

1 3 5 7 9 10 8 6 4 2

Design by Cerise Steel • Text set in Marselis Pro

The artwork in this book was created digitally using photoshop and a Wacom Cintiq.

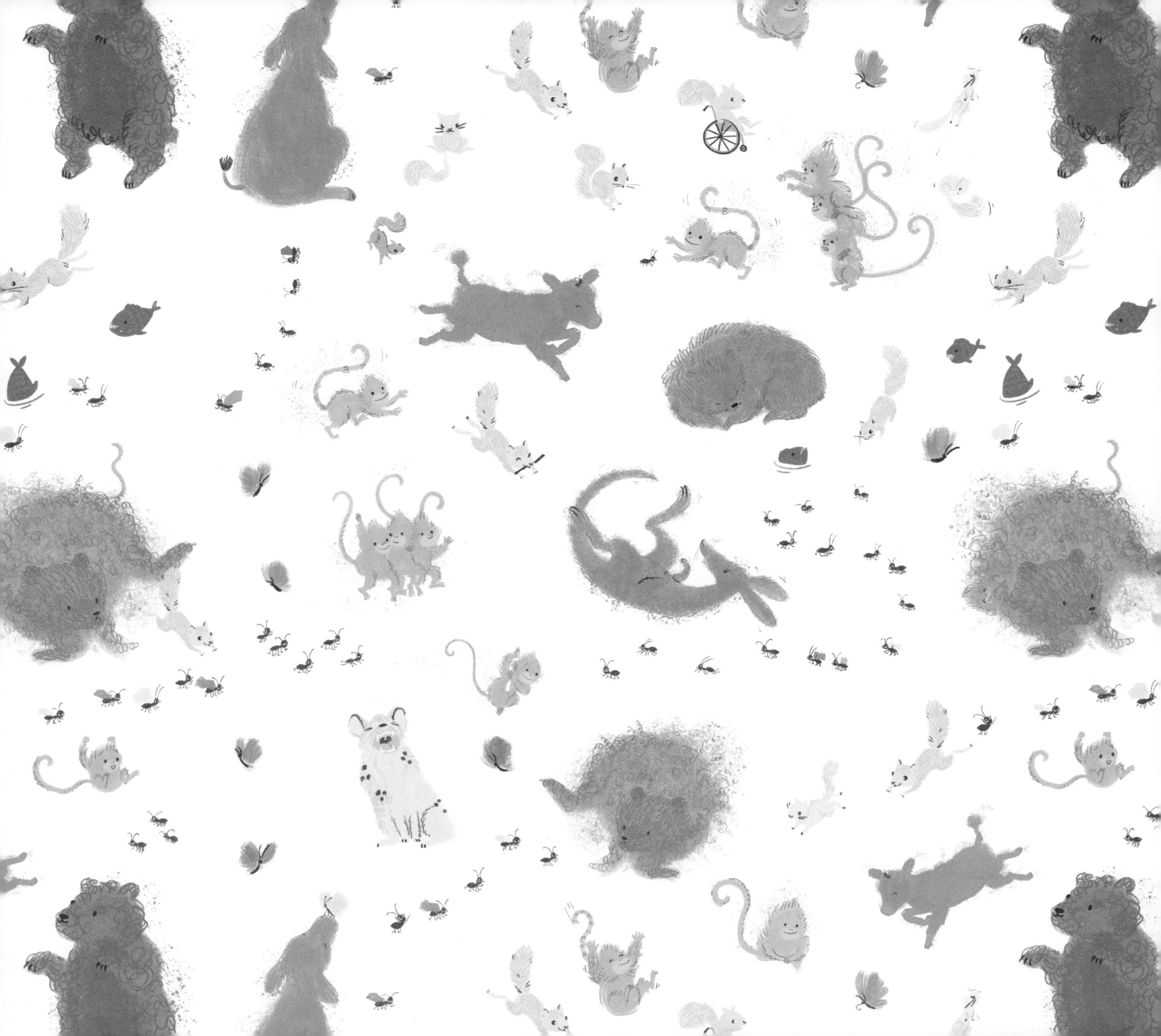

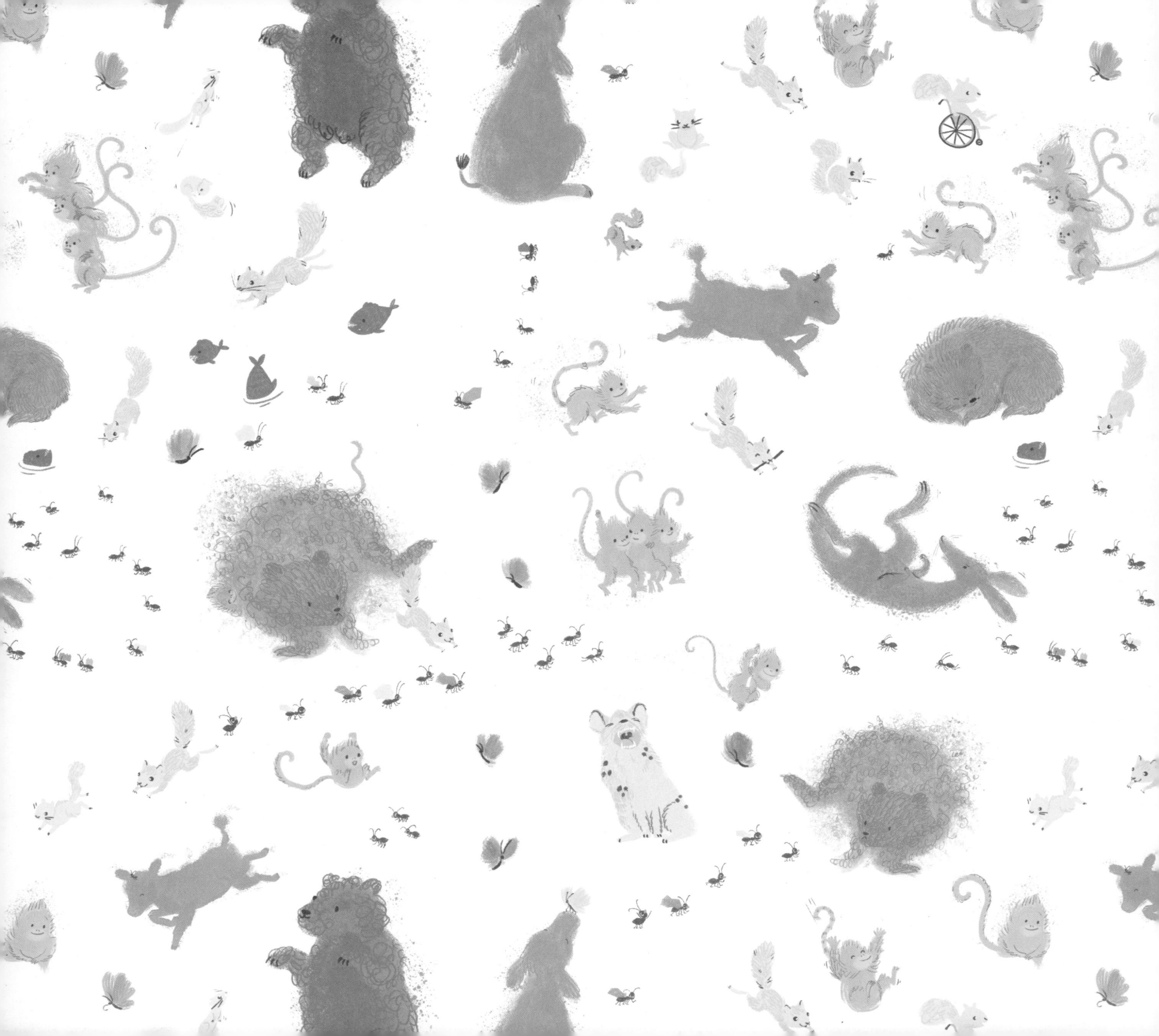